The NEW Small Person

Lauren Child

CANDLEWICK PRESS

To
Beatrice
and
Angelica
love
from
Lauren

First U.S. paperback edition 2018

Library of Congress Catalog
Card Number 2014939346

ISBN 978-0-7636-7810-4 (hardcover)
ISBN 978-0-7636-9974-1 (paperback)

18 19 20 21 22 23 APS 10 9 8 7 6 5 4 3 2 1

Printed in Humen, Dongguan, China

This book was typeset in Zine Slab.

Candlewick Press
99 Dover Street
Somerville, Massachusetts 02144

visit us at www.candlewick.com

FSC
www.fsc.org
MIX
Paper from
responsible sources
FSC® C101537

Elmore Green started off
        life as an only child,
as many children do.
He had a room all to himself,
and everything in it was his.

He was very proud
    of his room.

He watched all his favorite cartoons on his own little TV set — no one ever changed the channel.

He could line up all his precious things on the floor and no one moved them ONE inch.

When his uncle Cecil gave him a jar of jelly beans,
Elmore could eat every single bean, all by himself—
in whatever order he liked.

There was no need to worry about anyone
eating the orange ones because
Elmore Green's parents
did NOT

eat

jelly beans.

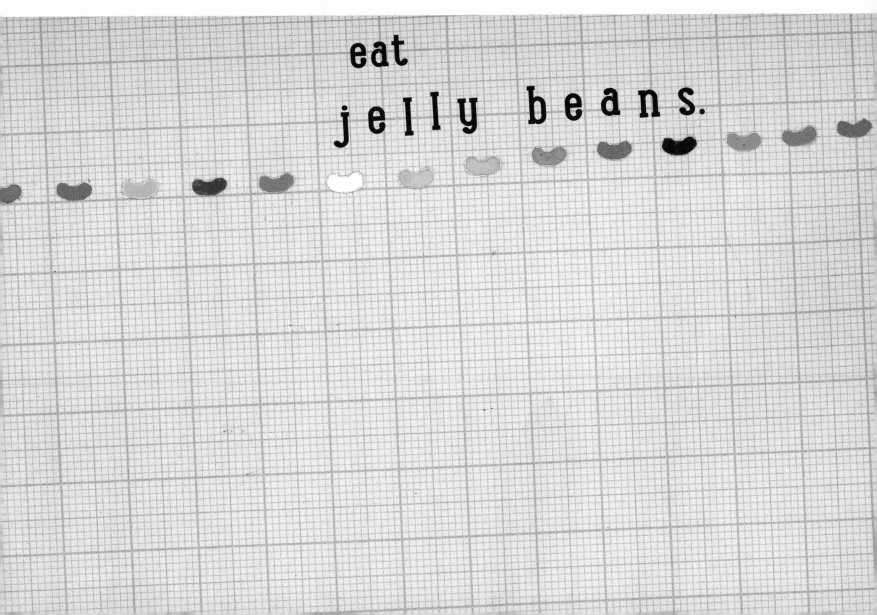

Elmore Green's parents thought he was simply
the funniest, cleverest, most *adorable*
person they had ever seen.

And Elmore Green liked that because
it is nice to be the funniest, cleverest,
most *adorable* person someone
has ever seen.

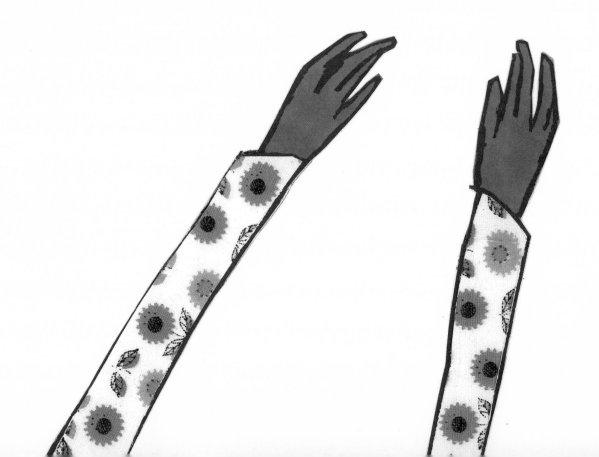

But
then
one day
everything
changed.

Somebody else came along.

The new person was small
and didn't do much, but still
people picked it up
          and *smiled* at it
and gave it things to chew.

They all seemed to
like it . . .

maybe

a little bit

MORE

than

they

liked

Elmore Green.

The new small person didn't like watching
Elmore Green's favorite TV cartoons
and would

squawk

until the channel
was changed.

Elmore did NOT find shows
for small people at all stimulating.

But everyone said
that the small person
couldn't help it
because it was

ONLY

small.

Sometimes the small person would come
into Elmore's room and knock things over
and sit on things that didn't want to be sat on.

Once it actually *licked* Elmore's jelly-bean collection,
including the orange ones. As anyone knows,
jelly beans that have been *licked*

are NOT nearly
so nice.

But everyone said Elmore

could NOT be angry because the small person was ONLY small.

Elmore Green wished
the small person
would go back to
wherever it
came from.

But Elmore's parents explained that this was NOT possible.

The small person got bigger.
And things got much worse.

One day Elmore found the small person wearing his fourth most favorite outfit.
Without asking.

"That's mine," said Elmore.
"It is NOT for small people."

"I want to be the same as YOU," said the small person.

But Elmore Green
did NOT want to be
the same as

someone

small.

The small person
followed
Elmore Green
everywhere.

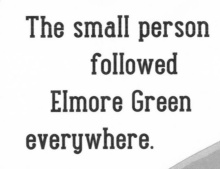

It wanted to sit
next to him; it wanted to
copy everything that Elmore did.
It wanted to be everywhere
that Elmore was.

"Where are you going, Elmore?"
said the small person.

"Nowhere," said Elmore.

"Can I come?" said
the small person.

When the small person
said things like this,
Elmore Green would go
and sit up a tree.

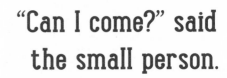

He

did

NOT

want

someone

small   following him around.

One awful day,
the small person
moved its bed into
Elmore Green's
room.

Now Elmore couldn't get away from it.
It was always there, looking at him.

Sometimes it would stretch out
its arms and say, "Huggle!"

But Elmore didn't want t

cuddle up to someone small. However, one night everything changed.

Elmore Green had a BAD dream. It was very upsetting —
a scary thing was *chasing* him, waving its grabbers
and gnashing its teeth.

Elmore screamed, and the small person
bravely got out of bed and
clung onto him.

"Go away, Scary!" shouted the small person.

It was nice
to have someone there
in the dark when
the scaries were around.

A few days later, Elmore Green was lining up all his precious things so they reached from his bedroom door all the way down the stairs.
It was a very long line of things.

The small person was amazed. "Oooh," it said.

"I could make them reach to the front door if I had more things," said Elmore.

"I have more things," said the small person.
"I have at least five or three things.
You can have them."

It felt good to have
someone there who understood
why a long line of things
was so
special.

The next evening, Elmore was laughing at the TV.

The small person looked at Elmore and then
at the TV, and then he laughed TOO.
   It was very funny.

More funny
somehow
with TWO people
laughing than just ONE.

Elmore opened his jar of jelly beans.
   "You can have a jelly bean
if you like, Albert."

His brother, Albert, smiled.
Elmore smiled back.

"Whichever
color
YOU like . . ."
said Elmore.

"except
orange!"